YOU COULD STOP IT HERE

STACY AUSTIN EGAN

[PANK] BOOKS

First Edition
1 2 3 4 5 6 7 8 9

Short selections may be reprodcued. To reproduce more than three pages of any one portion of this book write to PANK at awesome@pankmagazine.com

Cover Art by Io Escu
Cover Photo by Graham Austin

Library of Congress Cataloging-in-Publication Data

ISBN 978-1-948587-02-0

PANK Magazine
PANK Books

To purchase multiple copies or book events, readings and author signings contact awesome@pankmagazine.com.

To Brendan:
My first, last, and best reader and my best friend.

YOU COULD STOP IT HERE

STACY AUSTIN EGAN

TABLE OF CONTENTS

You Could Stop It Here

This is the moment you have the chance to avoid all consequences and not become involved. This is a part where you have choices. Make no mistake. There are choices. He will be in his office, and you will have a question about your British Literature and Culture paper on "*A Clockwork Orange* and the Youth Revolt in Novel and Cinematic Form." Just ask the question and don't sit down when he invites you to, and don't sit there and tell him how you loved the way he incorporated Kate Bush's song into his lecture on *Wuthering Heights*. Don't talk about how *Remains of the Day* made you cry.

This is a cliché. A student/professor relationship is trite and overdone, and you'd be stupid to think that you were the first, so don't stare at the stack of The Clash albums that are serving as a paperweight on his desk as a way to avoid staring at him because it's transparent and conveys desire more than if you looked right at him. You'll look vulnerable when you curl up in that university issued office chair and press your knees against your chest and feel your heart beat against your thighs. Better not to sit down in the first place.

Honestly, demonstrating that you are well-read does not make you seem in control or grown up or even self-assured. You think you are those things, of course, but just wait.

Don't believe me? Fine. When he says he's going to find a cup of coffee and asks if you want to join, forget about your plans with Sam to browse the bookstore on St. Mark's and say *yes*. Compliment him on his New School tie tack and think to yourself how he looks sort of like a British, better version of Tom Cruise.

When you find yourself sitting across from him in a booth at that deli with a forgettable name on Broadway and 4th, go ahead and nod sympathetically when he tells you about how he and his wife have been separated for several months now. Don't think about how several means two and separated does not mean divorced.

Listen, the way that you're wadding your napkin up into a tight little ball is a dead giveaway: You are terrified, and he knows it will only take one suggestion to reel you in. You should be thinking about how there is a different girl in every James Bond novel-- that's a life lesson straight from Ian Fleming. It doesn't matter how pretty or smart you are, but go ahead, tell him you would love to see that first edition of Oscar Wilde's plays, and take the 6 with him from Astor Place to 33rd, and be charmed when he swipes his metro card— twice.

*

In his apartment, talk about the picture of lady justice stripped bare above his bookcase; ask him about his time at Pembroke and Wolfson. Stupidly say, *I didn't know you wrote books*, and pull the hardback edition about forging British culture off of the shelf. Slowly run your fingers over the smooth cover with a time lapse photograph of a single 1940s AEC tank under an artillery ridden night sky, and let him tell you about his fascination with war culture and literature and how Harvard University Press is also publishing his next book.

If you are already at this point, you should ask to borrow that, by the way. It's a hundred and twenty five dollars on Amazon, and when things are all said and done, he won't ask for it back.

You have little to contribute here. These are the facts that make up your life: a high school diploma and not quite two years of college, a box of a room in Greenwich Village with an exposed brick wall and an air mattress on top of an Ikea loft bed, and a roommate who brings home someone different most weekends (guys and girls).

But tell him anyway. Let him convince you that you are interesting, that it's all so interesting. When he offers you a drink, don't say sure, and don't stare at the decanter like you have never seen one before, and don't make a horrible face because you've never tasted brandy.

Listen now, this is another point that you could walk away. You could just say, "Thanks for the drink, I'll see you on Monday," and you could go out into the February night, so cold it burns cheeks and fingers, and find someone closer to twenty. New York is a huge city, and there are a lot of guys in all of those taxicabs.

If you do stay though, know that this is what will happen: he will ask you about your weekend, and you will start talking about that Dresden Dolls concert you went to and how fun it was, and suddenly it will feel hot, and you will find yourself taking off your scarf, and then his arm will be around your shoulders, and you will move into him and exhale, and you will like how you fit in the crook of his elbow, and that is how you know you are really in trouble. You are going to become uncomfortable then, and you will finish that brandy, even though you don't like it. He will ask you to find a Dresden Dolls song, and you will

6

pull up "Shores of California" on his laptop, and he will rub his hand over your thigh, and before you know it, he will pull you closer, and the two of you will be kissing, and his hand will be cradling the back of your head, and you won't know what you're supposed to do with your hands, which should be yet another indication that you aren't ready for this; but go ahead, ignore your intuition.

See how good it feels to have someone taking off your skinny jeans after a cup of coffee and a subway ride. This is not *An Affair to Remember*, and you're no Deborah Kerr. You're supposed to be an adult, so if you have let it go this far, don't feel shocked that it's happening. This is what you were expecting, isn't it? Only it won't be anything like what you expected.

You didn't shave your legs or anything. You have only slept with two people, and you have no idea what you're doing. Before this, you didn't even think about how people can have sex standing up, but that's where you're going to be: against a wall. It's not like *Pride and Prejudice;* this is the way it works, satisfied? And it's going to hurt, honestly, because you're too nervous for foreplay to have done much, and you're going to be too terrified to say that it hurts, and you haven't learned how to really want it yet. He's going to kiss you all over your neck, and it's going to feel sort of frantic and rushed. He will ask if you're on the pill, and you won't come; he'll offer to go down on you, but that idea is petrifying: this is a person you have to look at every Monday, Wednesday, and Friday morning.

After, you will be standing there naked in the light of his reading lamp, and he's going to give you more brandy and hail a cab for you and pay the driver. There's not any intimacy or staying over. There's only that taxicab smell that you're going to forever associate with feeling empty and used.

*

On Monday, he's going to catch you off guard with a question about *Lucky Jim* in front of the class, and you're going to feel flushed, though you actually know the answer. Can other people tell that you have slept with him? Fucked would be the appropriate word here. He fucked you. Think about that sentence. No wonder you can't concentrate on this lecture. Maybe the TA will explain it later. She's sort of a bitch though. Wonder if he's been with her too? Think about how that's all anyone really is looking for: someone to sleep with, but that wasn't what you were looking for. You only wanted him to want you.

After class, he's going to ask to see you in his office. The high of that will make you dizzy all the way to the elevator.

Coincidently, he has an extra ticket to *Who's Afraid of Virginia Wolff?* This is what you thought you wanted, isn't it? Seriously though, he's twenty years older than you, and you really have nothing to wear. You could stop it here. Curiosity is captivating and so is the way he looks expectantly at you, his coffee cup the only thing between your bodies, but say you have plans, say you're scared shitless, say anything. Don't give him that half smile that men have learned to interpret as a yes. Imagine, from his perspective, how easy it looks to manipulate you, voiceless and hollow, into whatever position he chooses.

Really, this is the part where things are going to become dangerous because he's going to tell you that you are beautiful, and it's so easy to become addicted to things like how he walks close to you or how he holds your arm right above the elbow to make sure you don't slip in the crystallized sleet, scattered on the pavement like bits of shattered glass.

Once you are at this point, it's too late to entertain thoughts of turning back; the next few months are going to seem like a dream that you can't get out from under, or one that you can't get over, take your pick.

*

Tread cautiously. Lie to your mother about how you are spending your time. When Sam calls to ask why you are missing free Monday movies at Cantor, Wednesday nights at Pour House, and Fridays at the same shitty bars on Waverly that take fake IDs, tell him you have to explain later. You are eating nineteen-dollar starter salads and fried Brie with seasonal chutney at Café Benjamin now and developing tastes you can't afford to have. Don't think about that though. Really, the less you think, the better from this point on.

Don't worry about whose calls he's taking when he goes into the hallway at eleven. Don't worry about those weekends when he doesn't call, and you find yourself listening to your roommate screwing someone who lives in Alphabet City or Brooklyn instead of curled up in his window seat with *The Satanic Verses* wearing only his undershirt, the smell of it clinging to you like something you were always meant to absorb.

Let yourself learn to love how long thread Egyptian cotton feels against bare skin and how it feels to come from just being touched in the dark, and what it feels like to really want for someone, so badly that it creates a little pain inside of you, but whatever you do, don't let yourself love things specific to him.

Don't fall in love with the way he dog ears your page and closes your book and pulls you on top of him. Don't confuse the lust you feel when he runs his fingers over your collarbone towards your breast in that agonizingly slow way for something deeper. Don't find yourself needing his hand on the small of your back in order to fall asleep. Know that you are a temporary matter, a short-lived affair to fill a gap in his life when his wife was sleeping with her instructor from Pilates on Fifth.

For this reason, it's a good idea to stay in touch with those friends you have been ignoring for the past six weeks. When you tell Sam what's really going on while eating the falafel he bought you for lunch at your old favorite restaurant, don't assume his concern is merely jealously. Think about listening when he says he's worried about you. Don't smile in that way he can't see through and say *oh it's fine…great, I mean*. Don't tell him about how amazing the sex is just to try to reassure yourself that what you're doing is right. Have the decency to realize that he likes you as more than just a friend.

When he looks at you sadly, don't reapply your lip-gloss, thank him for the falafel, and say you have to run. Think about how good it would feel to tell someone about your fear and how you carry it with you all the time, a perfect thing that you're afraid to destroy.

*

This will change you; know that too. You will know your body in different ways, be hyper aware of the weight of your breasts, your range of flexibility, the freckles on the back of your neck that no one ever noticed until him. You will develop a craving for brandy and Muscato, a love for Mozart, an inability to concentrate without hearing some kind of background noise, like the way he clicks his pen while grading papers, or drums his fingers against his keyboard when he can't think of what to type.

Don't expect this to change him. He is not malleable in the way that you are, isn't waiting to be molded into new contours and curves. He has simply learned how to fill his time, and he is comfortable with the shape his life already takes. You may be enticing, and pretty, and stimulating, but don't underestimate the power of comfortable, and know that you won't be that. Not for him.

*

His wife's name is Elaine, and there is a picture of her on one of the bookcases in the study. She is beautiful in the way that older women are, a way that you might become, but not for a long, long time. Her skin is freckled from too much sun, but it looks soft from what you can tell. Her thick, black hair is pulled back, and she is laughing at a joke you probably wouldn't understand. There is a sexuality about her that shows through in the fullness of her lips, the accentuation of her eyes, the way that she leans against that stone fountain with one hip slightly more forward than the other, the way her thighs fill her jeans.

The photo is from some vacation they took; you don't know where. Add it to the list of things you don't know, of private things, of things that happened before you were even an idea, of things that make up the intertwining of two people's lives of which you are only a small, short interruption.

When March turns to April, don't register for his class next fall. Don't read too much into the fact that his doorman knows you by name or that those pearl earrings that he buys you for your twenty-first birthday are from Tiffany's. And no, it doesn't matter that he signed the card "With Love."

Love shower sex, counter sex, couch sex, but don't love him. Don't become too accustomed to the way it feels to lie on top of him while he strokes your hair or to stretching out between his legs. Don't develop a need for him. Needs create voids where we should have more of ourselves. Maybe it would help to know that going in. Maybe it would help if you knew yourself going in.

If you looked for the signs of distancing, perhaps it wouldn't hurt so much when things come to an end. Notice then how he takes walks around the block and doesn't invite you to come, how he showers now without waking you up, the way he doesn't ask the doorman for messages in front of you anymore. Pay attention to the indents that you both make in his king size Tempur-pedic mattress growing further and further apart. Note how he calls you darling less and less, how he seems more and more agitated, how he snaps at you for leaving the orange juice out on the counter.

Know that you're playing a very adult game: the rules are strange, and, of course, it never turns out fair.

In early May, when he asks you to come to his office, know that it isn't about your paper on *The Importance of Being Earnest*. People have a way of ending things in the places where they start them.

Don't remember him like this, sitting in his chair with his stupid Mont Blanc pen in his hand telling you *Elaine and I are going to work things out.* This does work out. For him. For her.

It's best to nod and try not to look like you're in shock. And whatever you do, don't let yourself cry.

Realize this is the only ending that ever is tacked on to stories like this; you could let it end.

*

For about twenty minutes, it's going to feel like the world is turning over on its side, and you have nothing to hold onto. You won't be able to feel people running into you as you make your way down Broadway, and you won't be able to hear the sounds of honking, of talking and shouting, of trucks, of shoes against concrete.

If you feel like you haven't created enough havoc in your life, here are some more bad ideas: take the 1 to Fulton Street and find yourself walking towards Water Street in a half conscious daze. Sit on a bench and watch a wrecking ball crash into the top of a building half a block away. Call Sam. End up in his dorm room smoking pot from the small blue glass pipe that you bought him for his last birthday, watching *The Godfather*, sitting on one of those horrible dorm furniture burlap love seats, and anxiously peeling at the wrapper on a can of Spaghetti O's instead of eating them. This is a long way down from Murray Hill.

Just because you know he will listen doesn't mean you should tell him everything while letting him hold you, so close you can feel the steady rise and fall of his chest, the rhythm of his breathing soothing in its predictability.

When he says *you should stay*, don't take a shower and curl up on his twin size bed with only a towel around you, the frayed edges barely covering your thighs. If you care about him and the way that he looks at you as if you are genuinely the most important thing, don't do that.

When he says *it'll be okay* and pushes your wet hair out of your face, know that intimacy is easy to initiate, but it's jagged and twisted and sometimes the edges are sharper than anyone knows to expect.

If you want to do some irreparable damage though, then disregard that shivering feeling running down your spine because being held and warm is the next best thing to feeling whole and okay. Sleep with him without considering him because it is something that you've learned how to do, because you want to see if making someone else feel good is the same as actually feeling good, because you're looking for distraction; be surprised that sex doesn't get rid of the sensation that you don't know who you've been since February, and that nothing feels right or comfortable or known.

Ask him to open the blinds; ask for a t-shirt; ask if it was okay.

Ask if he can get you a Xanax from someone in the dorm, and when he comes back to the room with one, take it. Feel heavy and so tired that you can't feel anything, which is really, if you were being honest, what you wanted all along.

Feel like you are numb and it's everything else around you that is melting. Don't think about the mess you've just created in his life. Think about yourself; you've become so good at that.

Sink into his chest and fight to keep your eyes open so you can watch the last of the day slip away.

Outside, the sun is setting, and for a moment, the Brooklyn Bridge looks like it's burning.

The Last Dare

Julie said, "What if in the future, you could sleep in a pod that would make it so you never aged or got cancer, but you'd have to sleep in it every night for it to work, and so you could never sleep next to a man?"

I painted one fingernail in Koala Berry and asked if it was the same as being immortal.

"No, no," Julie said. "You'd still die. You'd just look perfect until you did." She was sprawled over her twin-sized bed: government textbook and notes open, though she hadn't bothered to actually study them yet.

On my side of the room, I scrunched my nose, pretending to contemplate. This was the warm up round in truth or dare. The first truth or dare had to be easy, but the second and last round could ruin your life. That's how we'd played the game for years, though this would be our last time. It was a Monday night, and I was supposed to be writing an essay on *Once and Future King* for Ms. Morgan.

"I'd take sleeping next to a man," I said. At fifteen, I knew nothing of wrinkles and didn't worry about cancer, but I'd already been counting down the days until I turned sixteen (the age at which our mother had convinced our father we should be able to date) for three years.

"You would," Julie scoffed.

I wanted nothing more than for my older sister to see my answers as right, but I shrugged like I didn't care. We shared a room but less and less since Julie had started attending college two months ago. My dad wasn't going to pay for a dorm on campus at UT-Austin when my sister "could very well drive," so Julie lived at home, but I felt like she was living her real life somewhere else; when she was gone, I imagined the extraordinary opportunities her journalism major and news anchor face would afford her: trips to Europe, her choice of boyfriends, perfect hair. I was envious of it, this future I'd created for her.

"Truth or dare?" I asked.

Julie picked truth. There was so much I wanted to know, but I had to phrase it carefully in order to get as many details as possible. I needed to have dirt on Julie because then she couldn't leave me behind. At least, that was a kind of game we'd play: I'd want to go to a party with her, and she'd pretend she was only letting me because I knew too much. It was a casual excuse she could give her friends for why I was tagging along.

"She'll ruin my life if I leave her," Julie was fond of saying, though we both knew I idolized her and wouldn't have.

"Have you smoked pot?" I asked.

She doodled a picture of a goat in her notebook, un-phased.

"I'm in college," Julie reminded me. "Everyone smokes pot."

I tried to imagine my sister in someone's dorm room smoking a joint. Our father was a paramedic with a career's worth of drugs gone badly stories. He liked to tell them at dinner on the nights when mom was out playing Bunko. Most of them involved the user dying in his arms or before he arrived at the scene. "That was someone's baby," he would say, which he literally said every time.

Julie reapplied her lipstick and highlighted a sentence in her book.

"It was already bolded," I pointed out.

She tossed her highlighter at my poster of Ryan Phillippe. "Truth or dare?" she asked.

I picked dare, even though it was risky. Julie was liable to get her revenge: make me run naked past Scott Gray's house, or worse, call him and confess my love (I did NOT love him, but he had a driver's license, and mom made me ride to school with him).

Instead, she reached for her binder. She had printed *GOVERN-MENT, DR. GILMORE* on a red piece of paper and slid it underneath the clear plastic cover; from behind the paper, she pulled out an envelope that simply read Tommy on the front. Tommy was my sister's high school boyfriend. He had been on a mission trip to Africa, and he took French class instead of Spanish. He impressed me, though he annoyed Julie with a series of un-offensive actions, such as being the first to hang up when she said she had to go or not remembering that she was on a diet for prom and couldn't eat pizza.

"I need you to meet Tommy at Garrison Park and give him this," she said, handing me the envelope.

"You know I can't drive," I said, though Julie had taught me, so I could serve as her designated driver from time to time.

Julie reiterated that this was why the game was called *Truth or Dare* not *Truth or Take Legal Actions*, and she gave me her license in case I got pulled over. I did like the idea of seeing Tommy and running a secret errand for my sister, but I couldn't let her see that I didn't think it was such a bad deal on my end.

"What's in there?" I asked.

"Please," she rolled her eyes. "It will ruin your life if you look." I had four fingernails painted: the pinky one was plain and still had dirt under the nail; I ran the key beneath it, scrapping it clean on my way down the stairs.

*

I exited Ben White and eventually pulled into Garrison Park just a mile or so from our house; the whole time, I could hardly feel my fingers, and I had to keep reminding myself to stop gripping the wheel. "You probably won't get arrested" was the best I could reassure myself. When I pulled in, I looked across the parking lot for Tommy for confirmation that this was the right place. I waited for an entire song, Ben Folds on the radio, before questioning if people actually waited in their cars or if only mothers, destined to carpool pick up lines, did that. I opted to casually lean against my sister's Honda Civic.

I didn't see Tommy, but I thought I heard crying. I shifted my weight from one foot to the other. Probably an animal whining, I thought, but the longer it went on, the more it sounded like a person. "Hello?" I said softly, then louder "Hello? Is someone there? Tommy?" The noise was coming from the back of the park, towards the pool. I locked the car and tucked the envelope with Tommy's name into my back pocket. When I was a kid, I used to think of a jump rope song whenever something scared me. I knew it was stupid, but I started thinking of it in my head: *One two, buckle my shoe, three four, open the door, five six, pick up sticks, seven eight, lay them straight.*

I got to the pool and pressed my hands against the gate.

"Is someone there?" I said, but the crying had stopped. "Nine, ten, a big, fat hen," I sang softly to myself.

"No one is ever here," Tommy said, approaching.

I screamed and jumped towards the fence, as if I could evaporate and end up on the other side. Tommy laughed. I didn't have the courage to turn around.

"You scared me," I said finally. "I heard someone over here."

"*One, two Freddy's coming for you, three, four better lock your door,*" Tommy sang mockingly.

I felt my cheeks flush hot. My hands were red and smelled like rust. I held them up like proof. "I'm not kidding," I said. "Someone was crying."

"Hey, I was just teasing you," Tommy said. He put a hand on my shoulder, and I worked up the courage to look at him, noticed how much he had changed since May. He had come by the house for Julie's

15

graduation party: mingled with our grandparents and played with our little cousins in the tree house outside our window that my dad had never taken down. But now, his dark hair and green eyes made it hard to turn away, and I felt guilty for looking when it was just the two of us, and I wasn't safe behind the glass where, even if he had seen someone, he wouldn't have known it was me.

"Oh," I said finally.

"You just look really nervous," he said.

He looked every bit an adult. I remembered when Julie started looking that way. I watched her sleeping on the couch one night, and she was this woman, with real curves and everything, and I was this stupid kid with hand-me-down jeans and a bra without an underwire. I watched her laying there, still my sister, but somehow, someone else too. I wondered if it would happen to me next and if it would hurt. I wanted it to happen; I felt like all I did was wait for it. Standing there with Tommy, I wondered if he could be the one to change me.

"I don't have a license yet," I said.

"Want to swim?" Tommy asked.

"Is it open?" I was surprised and secretly thrilled that he wanted to prolong our meeting.

"It's a pool. It has water in it." His statement of the obvious embarrassed me enough to make me consider leaving. As if Tommy would adhere to some posted pool hours. He started climbing the fence, and I struggled to follow.

"Maybe you should take this," Tommy said, offering me his hand.

I wondered if they were both playing a joke on me: maybe the envelope was just a ploy to get me grounded for life, or maybe Julie was simply testing my faithfulness. I took his hand in mine like it was a trick: carefully, still deciding whether or not it was firm enough to hold on to. Ignoring a "No Trespassing" sign should feel dangerous, I thought, but it was oddly disappointing how easily we got in; it didn't feel like trespassing should: no alarm going off, no dogs barking at us from the other side of the fence; we didn't tear our clothes on anything or sustain any injuries. I felt like breaking rules should have immediate consequences.

When it didn't, the whole world, everything just felt off, like if you got away with this, something else was coming for you later.

Tommy started to take off his shirt, and then, I noticed something in the pool. At first, I thought it was dead animals, but it was just sneakers, about thirty pairs floating in the water.

"Weird," Tommy said.

"What are they?" I asked.

"Shoes," he said.

Again, I felt my throat closing. I hadn't meant literally, but I was hyper aware of how I was coming across to him. I didn't want to be a child to him: this night, it had to be important because maybe it was the thing standing between who I was and who I wanted to be; I could be as brave and beautiful and daring as Julie if Tommy would just see me that way.

He took off his shirt and pants and jumped in. I stared at the way his back dipped in right above the line of his smiley-face Joe Boxers. I hadn't even considered not having a swimsuit. I unbuttoned my jeans and shimmied them off and felt thankful that I had worn one of Julie's bras: the Victoria's Secret kind with the padding. I unclipped Julie's tortoise shell barrette, borrowed but not returned, and shook out my long, brown hair. Tommy didn't look at me, which made me feel both relieved and offended. The water was dark and cold. I couldn't decide if it was dangerous or peaceful; back then, I didn't think about how something could be both.

I swam out to the center of the pool, and Tommy and I started grabbing the sneakers by the shoelaces and placing them on the edge. They were all sizes: men's and women's lace-ups, children's shoes with Velcro, Nikes and New Balances and Converse. There was even this one pair of toddler shoes. It felt good to have something to do: a clear objective that I could easily meet. Julie's bra absorbed pool water, and in that moment, I felt heavy but confident in the weight of my temporary assets.

"Julie's taking me to a Pearl Jam concert for my sixteenth birthday," I said, extra emphasis on my upcoming impressive sounding age. I hopped up on to the edge of the pool.

"I know," Tommy said. "She told me." He went underwater and swam the length of the small pool.

It made me defensive. I wanted there to be special things that only Julie and I knew. I wanted him to need me to tell him things. I flipped over one of the shoes. On the bottom, in black marker, someone had written *HOW*.

"Hey, come look at this," I said. He swam to the ledge. I felt the hair on my arms stand up straight.

On the bottom of each shoe either the word *HOW* or *MANY* was written in black marker in all caps. Left shoes had the *HOW*, right had *MANY*. We turned over all the shoes: *HOW MANY, MANY, MANY, HOW MANY, MANY HOW* stared back at us.

"It's Freddy Kruger level creepy," I said; the flirtatiousness of my tone surprised even me. I had only ever kissed Scott Gray on a dare, and Jeremy Mills touched my boobs over my shirt last year at Playland Skate. I didn't even know that I could sound like I knew how to do more than kiss with my mouth closed.

Tommy raised an eyebrow at me. "Maybe it's some kind of art project," he said. "You know, like, experimental? I'm taking a course about it this semester."

I was simultaneously completely impressed with his knowledge of the world and mortified by my own inability to use the terms course or semester nonchalantly.

"Should we leave?" I put my hands on my thighs and leaned over. I felt suddenly sick, and the chlorine smell made it worse. Out of the pool, I was shivering, and suddenly, swimming in our underwear in late October felt pretty stupid.

"Because of the sneakers?"

"Well what if they belong to someone; someone that's you know." I looked around nervously and finished in a whisper, "Someone that's coming back?"

"For their lame, soggy sneakers?"

Tommy threw one into the pool, as if to demonstrate how worthless they were. In high school, he was the pitcher for the baseball team. *Baseball has a horribly long season,* Julie had said; *never date a player.* He looked strong; I would kiss him with my mouth open, I realized. Not like Scott Gray. The shoe just floated there by itself. It looked lonely, the way the light from underwater shined on it bobbing face down, the laces slowly reaching for the bottom, the water a cocoon.

Tommy retreated to his jeans and took out a carton of cigarettes and a lighter. "You want one?" he asked.

I said sure, though I did not. When he sat next to me, I focused on inhaling and tried not to focus on the open space in his boxer shorts. I started feeling light headed and nauseous and stood up, which was the wrong choice.

"It's freezing," I said. Tommy offered me his old letter jacket. I sat down on one of the lounge chairs, wrapping it around my shoulders and liking the heaviness and his smell (sweat, dirt, and grass on top of leather) that hugged in around me. It was a perfect moment: I could feel myself becoming cooler right before I went and ruined it.

"I think I might throw up," I said.

"I have something in the car," Tommy said. He left without waiting for my response.

I didn't want to be alone, but definitely, I also didn't want to puke in front of Tommy. I watched him jump the fence again. I took the envelope out of my jeans. I wasn't supposed to open it, but I started thinking about it and decided knowing something Tommy didn't and being bold would outweigh Julie's potential (and only if she found out) wrath. I tried tearing it carefully, so maybe he wouldn't notice.

I reached inside and pulled out a picture the size of a Polaroid. It looked like a negative: black and white and shiny. At first, I thought it didn't look like anything, just this white light in the center of blackness. Then it occurred to me that it looked like an ultrasound. At the top it said "Finnigan, Julie A. 9 weeks, 3 days." It had Friday's date. I felt like I couldn't hear anything over my own blood rushing to my head. I held the ultrasound towards the pool's light. It looked like an acorn, not a human. Julie had done something I wasn't capable of, and it felt like the worst betrayal I could have imagined: the final illustration that she had grown up and left me behind.

I leaned over the lounge chair and threw up, closed my eyes, and tried to feel something other than dizzy. I stayed hunched over like that for a minute; my vision was making things spin, but I felt like it was the world that was moving differently.

"What are you doing?"

I opened my eyes. A man in a baseball cap and a hoodie shined his flashlight directly at me.

I looked up into the light and pulled Tommy's jacket close around me. "Uh, swimming," I said, not as if it were obvious, but like I too was completely floored by it.

"Pool's closed."

"Sorry." I sat up. He seemed too serious about it. He started pacing back and forth against the fence.

"I should report this," the man yelled.

"I don't think you should," I said, but really, getting arrested was starting to look preferable to what I had been sent to do.

It wasn't until I noticed something in his hands that it occurred to me to panic. I immediately thought he had a gun. I thought he may rape me, an idea I got from watching too many opening five minutes of *Law and Order* episodes with my mother before she would say (of all Special Victims Unit episodes) "Jamie, this one isn't appropriate for you," as if any of them ever were.

"Who are you," the man asked, moving closer to the gate. The question felt unanswerable, so I just sat there, though I don't think he meant it in a philosophical way. He pushed the latch up, and I realized that it had been unlocked this whole time. His eyes are what really scared me: the skin underneath them looked like it had been rubbed raw. His face looked too red and old for his body.

"You better go away," I said. "My boyfriend's coming back, and you better go." I liked using that word, *boyfriend*. It felt powerful, sacred, but the man still pushed open the gate and stepped through. I could see Tommy running towards us. I backed away towards the deep end side of the pool and yelled his name. He ran through the open gate. I said his name again like a warning.

"What's going on?" Tommy asked.

He didn't look like such an adult to me now, just standing there in his yellow underwear holding a bottle of Gatorade.

"There's no problem here," Tommy said. He rolled his shoulders back like he was ready to take care of anything, but I could feel my skin, now stiff from the chlorine, and I knew that everything we were before, none of it mattered now. I was looking to him to make this okay, but he was swinging his arms like he was warming up for a game of flag football. I'm going to die here, I thought, more certain now.

The man's eyes met Tommy's. I watched Tommy move around him in a half circle with his arms out, a strange dance that he did not seem to really know.

"Back off man!" Tommy yelled; it echoed, but there was no one except us to hear it.

The man threw something at me, and I screamed. It barely missed my head and then bounced on the wire fence and off the concrete: a man's sneaker.

"You kids are idiots," the man said.

Tommy stood behind me, his hands on my shoulders. I couldn't even move; I was shaking so bad.

Tommy whispered, "Do you know what he wants?"

I shook my head. I did not know what anyone wanted. I actually longed to be in Geometry class.

"Calm down," Tommy said. "It was just a sneaker." I think he even smiled. Maybe I would have even loved him for it if I hadn't been so angry.

"My son died here," the man yelled. He voice softened then, "A little boy, Colin. This past summer."

"We didn't know," I said. I started to think back on my dad's stories from the summer: there had been so many about kids drowning over the years. Maybe this man had to be tranquilized. Dad says, every now and then, death can make a person rage, make someone forget he's a person even.

"Sorry," Tommy said. The wind blew. I backed against him then stepped forward, afraid of the stranger and of Tommy's body equally.

The man started throwing the shoes back in the pool one by one. Tommy moved in front of me. I was pushing back into the fence so hard, the wires, even through Tommy's jacket, left diamond marks on my skin.

"A lot of people drown in pools," the man said. "Every year, and no one does anything. Then they leave a pool unlocked at night; just leave it totally open for two more dumb kids like you."

"We didn't actually know it was unlocked," I said, as if the fact that we thought we were breaking in made it more forgivable.

"This is important to me now," the man said.

Tommy whispered "climb," but I stood frozen. I thrust the ultrasound photo into his hand.

"Here," I said, meanly. "This is yours."

He squinted his eyes to look at it. "What?" he said quietly, as if he didn't want the man to hear.

The man threw another shoe. It hit me in the shin. I started crying but not because it hurt.

"I *told you* I heard someone," I said to Tommy. I felt my right foot in a hole in the fence and then my left. It hurt without shoes, and that pain was reassuring. On the other side, I ran and didn't turn around.

"Jamie," Tommy called after me. "Wait!"

He was faster, and I was only ahead because he had stopped to look at the ultrasound; when he made it to the car, he grabbed my arm and pulled me towards him.

"I wasn't supposed to open it," I said. I held my hands to my ears; I thought he would start yelling.

He let go of my arm. He'd gripped too hard, and it would leave a mark. "This is a baby?" he asked, waving Julie's ultrasound, wrinkled and stained now, at me frantically and pressing me against the hood of her car.

I'd never felt so angry in my life. "What do you think it is?" I said.

"What's wrong with you?" he said softly.

"I liked you," I yelled at him, pushing him away.

The shove had hardly any effect. He stood up straight and held up his hands to show he wouldn't push back.

"Is this her idea of some joke?" I asked. Then it made me angrier that I was asking him what he thought about her when I should be the one to know her best of all. I was crying, but I tried to make it seem like it was because my shin was hurt.

"It's not my fault," he said.

"Whose fault is it?" I scoffed. "She didn't do it to herself."

"Dammit," Tommy said. "We were careful. I fucking swear it."

His statement would lead me to use condoms and birth control pills together for all of my young adult life. I'd been hoping to find bravery that night, but instead, I'd become more convinced that every rule I ever broke would come back to punish me in the most unpredictable way. It was a fear that took years of my life to break, and even now, it resides with me in moments of helplessness when I most want to assign a cause to the blame.

When I answered only with a glare, he said, "Stay here," as if I were a small child lost in a shopping mall.

I half expected him to not come back, but he did. He gave me my purse and clothes and pressed Julie's keys gently in my hand. He had dressed again. The ultrasound stuck out of the front of his shirt like a pocket square. He held his hand over it as if pledging allegiance.

"At least we can get home now," he said, more to himself than to me.

I nodded. We could.

I could picture Julie still in bed waiting for me to come back. I could see her lying on her back, staring up at the ceiling. I tried to imagine her in our room with a baby, rocking it or singing to it. She wasn't gentle like that yet though.

"Please don't look," I said, as I gave back Tommy's jacket and pulled my clothes on over my wet skin.

"Tell her I'll call her," he said, facing away towards our cars.

"Tell her I..." he started to add something but stopped. "I'll call her," he said again, as if convincing himself.

We started cars; I checked the mirrors before I backed up. The last time I ever saw Tommy, it was in my headlights: his hands pressed against his forehead, his elbows lying on the horn.

*

A week later, I would be the one to take Julie for her D&C. She hadn't been sleeping well, and she'd missed a major test, was worried she might fail at least one class. Tommy hadn't returned her calls, and it wasn't okay to say his name anymore. I never told her everything about that night: the creepy man, the swimming, the shoes. I kept it all for myself like a strange dream about a girl I once wanted to be.

I read my World History book in the waiting room and pretended this wouldn't change anything. On the way home, I told her about Henry the VIII, his six wives, and his daughters. I kept talking, anxious to fill the silence.

"I've heard all this before," Julie said, shutting her eyes and lying against the passenger seat of her own car. I wanted to be in her head, close to her, but all I could be was on the outside and desperately searching for a way in.

When we got home, we'd have to park around the corner so my dad, who worked the night shift, or the neighbors wouldn't see me drive, and I'd have to make up a lie about Julie feeling sick. She walked strangely because of the maxi pad and the lingering effects of anesthesia, and we stopped several times on the way to the front door.

"Julie has food poisoning," I yelled in lieu of hello, ushering her up the stairs.

"You girls and Chinese food," Dad said, not looking up from the paper. It would have never worked with mom.

When Julie finally made it up the stairs, she collapsed in bed. I thought I should leave her to sleep, but she opened her eyes.

"Which of the daughters got to be Queen first?" she asked

"Mary," I said "the older one."

"That's good," she said, her eyes falling shut. "That's right."

I turned to go, but she said, "Could you start at the beginning? Start with Catherine of Aragon," and I sat on the edge of her bed and combed her hair with my fingers while I talked.

Outside, our tree house ladder was missing the first and last of its wooden steps. When we were younger, we used to pretend it was a castle: our palace was far away, and it never had the same name twice. We got in trouble once for building a moat around the tree. We were proud of it, even though our parents were angry. When they'd made us fill it in, Julie had said very confidently: *I don't think it was a mistake*. Before we grew up, we understood how to protect ourselves, and we acted on our impulses with the self-assurance that we'd always be safe because there was no mess, nothing we'd ever made, that couldn't be undone.

Say at Me You Are My Friend

Agatha places her ice cream scoop in soapy water, leans against the crush-in board, and adjusts the bandana covering her hair. From the side room, Kirk stops slicing strawberries and gives her a long look. She can feel his gaze, though she pretends to be oblivious to it. "Hey, don't lean on that," he says, and he moves to wipe the whole board down with a sponge, scrubbing hard where Agatha's elbow had rested. "This is for mauling ice cream with toppings, not slouching on." He flicks her long brown ponytail. "Your hair," he says to her, "is not in a bun."

Agatha loves him. From the corner of the parlor, Kirk's girlfriend, Megan, the sole customer glares.

"Jesus," Patrick says from the cash register. "Someone has their panties in a wad since becoming shift manager."

Agatha doesn't dare laugh. She fixes her hair into a neat bun and goes into the side room to wash her hands. It's a Tuesday night, and the store is empty, save for Magic Mountains, Patrick and Agatha's code name for Megan.

"I don't know what you're always daydreaming about," Kirk says to Agatha. "But if you really have nothing to do, you could help me slice these."

"Really?" she says, not hiding her happiness. Patrick rolls his eyes. He has already told Agatha, twice, how pathetic her passive attempts at flirting are. Violating health codes on purpose, he said, was an all time lame strategy for attracting someone.

From the corner booth, Megan watches Agatha and Kirk disappear into the side room and noisily slurps the ice cream off her wooden sample spoon. Megan has gained at least five pounds since Kirk became shift manager two weeks ago. Kirk once told Agatha that he thought Megan looked just like Bettie Page, but the only resemblance Agatha saw was the short bangs and exposed cleavage. Megan was no pin up girl. This fact did little to diminish the jealously Agatha felt over the fact that Kirk had named a sundae: Megan's Mocha Magic Mountains. In Kirk, Agatha saw everything the boys at her high school lacked: world knowledge, culture, a car, and maybe, the power to help her lose her virginity.

Agatha is not very good at slicing strawberries, and everyone at Amy's knows it. She's too careful with the knife, and slices one strawberry for Kirk's four.

"Watch," he says, holding his hand under hers as he slices.

Agatha can pay attention to nothing about his technique. She just makes a memory of his hands, confident and sure, and thinks about how she wants him to put one on her shoulder, or bat at her hair again, or touch her in any way that says, *hey, we are here together, and I see you too, the way you want to be seen.*

Megan comes up to the counter, clears her throat, and taps the heel of her stiletto against the tile. "Darling," Magic Mountains calls. "I'm headed home, okay? Call me when you're on your way."

"Uh-huh," Kirk says, not shifting his focus from the strawberries, or, Agatha hopes, maybe it's the feel of her hand under his own that is holding him there.

"I'll stay awake for you," Megan says.

Patrick feigns throwing up into the deep freeze and Agatha laughs.

Megan makes an exasperated gesture towards the ceiling. "Thanks for the goodbye kiss, Kirk," she says.

Patrick puckers up and leans over the sneeze guard, pressing his hands into the crush-in board.

"Grow up," Megan says. She sashays towards the glass door; the cowbells attached to the top ring as she slams it behind her.

"I think you're in trouble," Patrick says.

"Nah," Kirk says. "I need to get stuff done; she knows how it is."

"Uh-huh," Patrick says. He eats some Nutter Butters that are supposed to be used for toppings straight out of display bin. Kirk glares at him.

Agatha says, "Use the tongs."

"I used them for something nasty earlier," Patrick says. He erupts into maniacal laughter and then uses the tongs to drop a Nutter Butter directly into his mouth.

"Beyond disgusting," Agatha says. Kirk sprays a can of Lysol in Patrick's general direction.

It is nine o'clock, and the three of them will be here at least four more hours. When the store is quiet, Agatha feels there is little more to do than ponder what life will feel like when something interesting happens.

Patrick paces behind the counter. He re-writes the quote selection for the "guess the movie quote and win a free topping" game at least eight times, updating Kirk on the changes. Kirk wants to use, "Boy, say at me you are my friend, so I will not die alone," from *Red Dawn*, but Patrick wants, "It's one thing to want someone out of your life, but it's another thing to serve them a wake up cup full of liquid drainer" from *Heathers*. Agatha votes with Patrick, feeling secure that her choice disguises the fact that she has dedicated fifteen minutes of every hour to just staring at Kirk. "Congratulations," Patrick says. "You are a member of the most powerful clique at school." Though he is scrawny, he has no trouble lifting Agatha off the ground and carrying her out to the lobby while they both chant "VIC-TOR-Y, VIC-TOR-Y!" Kirk announces that he has the urge to purge.

The cowbells ring a few times throughout the night: a couple of UT kids, a few women from next door's pregnancy massage class, and a Thundercloud Subs employee. Almost everyone takes their orders to go or outside onto the picnic tables. The store is over air-conditioned in the summer, and only the three of them are warm enough; the heat that radiates from the deep freeze hangs around them, making them anxious for outside air. Agatha's jeans are always sticking to her by the end of the night, the smell of heavy whipping cream has become her perfume, and the pain in her wrists is a strange source of pride.

Half past midnight, after losing three rounds of rock-paper-scissors to Agatha, Patrick takes out the trash. She begins counting the tips from their "Will Scoop for Food" jar and thinking about being in California with Kirk, that the experience will be transformative enough to make her brave: the kind of girl who could wear a bikini and pin her hair back with a rose.

Something is strange, even in the way that the bell rings signaling Patrick's return. Agatha looks up from the crumpled bills in her hands and sees Patrick enter with two men. Both have ski hats pulled down to their eyes, dark sunglasses, and heavy beards, and one holds a gun out far in front of him, like he isn't really sure what to do with it.

The heat feels like a wall, and Agatha can hear her breath in and out and feels her knees come close to buckling. There is supposed to be a code word for a robbery. If she says it, Kirk can exit out the back and call the police, but whatever the word is, it doesn't come to her now.

"Need strawberries?" Kirk says, coming out with a large bin full. It's too late now, and the man with the gun says, "Get your asses down on the ground!"

Agatha drops in front of the deep freeze, and Kirk scrambles to sit directly in front of her.

The man points his gun at Patrick. "Not you," he says. "You get the money."

"I'm the shift manager actually," Kirk says, attempting to stand up.

"I don't give a raccoon's tooth who you are," the man says.

27

"Don't move unless I tell you to."

Patrick works steadily; he moves to the register and empties everything into one of the paper sacks they keep for to-go orders. Agatha can't see much from behind Kirk, except for the man that hasn't said anything. He bounces on the balls of his feet and keeps his eyes on the ground, his hands in the pockets of a black leather jacket, out of place in summer.

"Move away from her," the man with the gun says to Kirk. "I wanna see your hands."

Agatha holds up her hands. For some reason, all she can think about is her pen pal, Howard, from second grade and about how he abruptly stopped writing. She recalls sending him a final letter: *Dear Howard, Isn't there anything left to say? Hello? Your Pal, Aggie,* but in a moment, the thought is gone.

"Jesus, don't point that at me. I'm going as fast as I can," Patrick says.

The man leans close to Patrick, who adds the tip money in and hands him the bag. "That's it man; I gave you what I got." He points to the empty divider in the cash register with one hand and holds the other up in surrender.

"What movie is that quote from?" The one that hasn't talked says.

Just then, the cowbells ring, and even just from the girly gasp, Agatha can tell it is Megan, a plate full of Mangia pizza in her chubby hands. She turns around to run, but the man with the gun surges ahead, reaches the door first, and locks it. He demands to know where the lights are, and he shuts them off, the neon "Sorry, we're closed" sign remains plugged in, their only source-of-light save for the street lamps.

"What do we have here?" he says, eyeing Megan's pizza.

Kirk stands up. "Leave her alone," he says. The man points the gun at Kirk and tells him to sit down.

"I was bringing my boyfriend some pizza," Megan wails.

"Is that deep dish Chicago style pizza?" the other one asks. Agatha presses her knuckles against her lips and struggles to hear over the hum of the freezers. Megan sits by the door whimpering.

"HEY!" the one with the gun says. "My buddy asked you a question. Yes or no, is that deep dish pizza?"

Agatha hears Patrick take a deep breath; he does not exhale.

"Yes," Megan says.

"Stop," Kirk says.

"Well," the other one says. "We can't let that go to waste. I'm thinking you're gonna wanna eat that." He takes the plate of pizza and sets it down on the table of the corner booth. "I'm gonna need to get this girl a soda!" He walks behind the counter and reaches out his hand to Agatha. "Come on sweetheart, how about a soda?"

Agatha picks up a cup, scoops in some crushed ice, and selects Dr. Pepper: Megan's favorite. She brings it over to her.

Kirk stands up again. "This is stupid," he says. "Take your money and go."

The man with the gun moves closer to the table and jabs his weapon between Agatha's shoulder blades. She can feel it, sharp and solid against her bones.

"I'll decide what's stupid," he says.

Dear Howard, she thinks, *you have missed your chance.*

Megan grabs her hand, maybe a reflex or maybe something more, but Agatha knows she can't leave now.

"May I, also have some pizza?" she asks.

The man with the gun laughs. "Look at this one! Skin and bones," he says, measuring Agatha's wrist between his pointer finger and thumb. "You help yourself."

"Skin and bones" the other one chuckles. Then he sings it like a song: *skin and bones, skin and bones. Bones and skin and skin and bones.*

Agatha takes gigantic bites of the pizza. She tries to telepathically communicate with Megan by looking into her gray eyes, the half circles of bleeding mascara accentuate them, and suddenly, Agatha sees the ways in which Megan actually does resemble Bettie Page, her lips forming that signature pout as she takes tiny sulking bites.

The man with the gun leans over Megan, and Agatha can hear him whisper, *"What's the matter with your pizza?"*

"She has a lactose intolerance," Agatha says; when a look of horror crosses the gun-holder's face, she fully believes she might have just gotten them both killed. In her peripheral vision, she sees Kirk pressed against the deep freeze, Patrick gripping his elbow, but in the dark, she can't see their faces.

"Why didn't you say so?" the other one asks.

"It's a sensitive subject," Agatha says. Suddenly, she seems to really grasp that her life is just beginning. She doesn't know why she never thought about it before, but everything there is to lose is outside of here…all the hours, days, and decisions she hasn't made yet seem to materialize in her mind. The man with the gun's voice shatters the idea of them before she can figure out what the questions are or ponder what her choices would be.

"Get the hell out!" he says to Megan. "This is a damned ice cream store!"

"Are you serious?" Megan says. She looks worriedly at Kirk and mouths *I love you* as the man with the gun escorts her roughly to the door, grabbing her pink sequined purse; he unlocks it, and, as if it were nothing

29

says, "Thanks for coming! Have a moo-licious day!"

The other one pulls Agatha up. "I'm gonna need some music," he announces. Patrick goes into the side room and turns on the stereo. It blares *The Cars Greatest Hits*, starting with "Shake It Up." The man holds Agatha close and slow dances with her. It takes all she has not to choke on the smell of him, which is a weird combination of armpits and oranges. He lifts his arm and she twirls under him: the movement and knowledge of what to do seems to come from somewhere outside of her. She recalls baring her soul to Howard in one particularly emotional letter she mailed shortly before her cousin's wedding: *Dear Howard, I hate dancing. And dresses.*

Patrick says, "Don't do anything you'll regret. She's just a kid." He swallows, as if to stop himself from adding more.

"We're just dancing," the other one says. "Are you jealous because I wouldn't dance all night with you?"

The man with a gun takes a seat in the booth, tapping his foot to the music. He finishes Megan's half of the pizza. "This is nothing to cry over," he says defensively. "But next time, order pepperoni."

The other one laughs, bearing his plaque-ridden teeth and gums. "How about that movie quote?" he asks Agatha.

She whispers, "It's from *Heathers*."

"What's that about?" he says.

"It's about…these girls named Heather."

Is the gun pointed at her? She really doesn't know. She hears Patrick's voice, "God, breathe Aggie." Her eyes are open, but all she sees is the checkered pattern of the floor. She tries to listen to Patrick, but all she hears is *Go to work! Do the move with quirky jerk!* She tries to remember all of the flavors they have right now: After Dinner Mint, Banana Cream Pie, S'mores, Peanut Butter Oreo, Chocolate Wasabi…she can't remember anything else, and after that, it's all nothing.

*

She wakes up on the tile. Patrick is holding a cold rag to her face, and Kirk is on the phone.

"You scared the life out of those guys. I think they thought you had a seizure or something," Patrick says.

Agatha has a raging headache. "Why'd they think that?"

"Maybe because Kirk yelled, 'Oh God, she's having a seizure or something!'" Patrick says.

"Is it *strawberry*?" Agatha asks. "The safe word?"

"It's *serendipity*," Patrick says.

Kirk hangs up the phone. "It's *Saratoga*," he says.

She doesn't know who starts it, but suddenly their laughter fills the store; it's a quiet choking at first, but their snickers slowly grow into a rhythm that they cannot contain. It hurts her stomach and sides: this strange and uncontrollable relief that comes with having not lost. And then they find themselves just staring at each other, waiting.

The blood rushes to Agatha's head as Kirk helps her off the floor, and she heads to the bathroom to get some wet paper towels. Nothing there seems familiar. There is so much written on the wall that she has never bothered to read. Next to a permanent marker drawing of a woman's bare breasts, someone has written *Own your pain, Own your joy, Own your LIFE*. Underneath, in red lipstick that is already smudged, *you can only own what you can control*. Mostly, there are just a series of initials and dates. Everyone needs to say they were here.

After talking to the police about clothing and heights and teeth and tones, Agatha retreats outside for some air. She sits on top of the picnic table squeezing her hands in the gap between her calves and thighs. It does not stop the trembling she feels within. She tries to focus on the hopscotch that someone drew with purple chalk in front of the store and wills herself to think of what it would feel like to play: two feet, left foot, two feet, right foot. She tries to make herself take long breaths and peels the dead skin off her bottom lip with her front teeth until it bleeds. All she wants to do is go home, apply for school, feel the rest of the year go by, and then go be someone else.

Kirk comes outside to lock up, the keys dangling from his pocket. Patrick follows behind him, grumbling about the stolen tips and his inability to buy cigarettes. Agatha didn't even notice the police leaving, but she suddenly realizes their car is gone. Tomorrow, the owner will meet them at the store to file an official report, and later, there will be more phone calls and the need for additional statements, but for now, it's just the three of them and the constant buzz of Guadalupe Street oblivious to it all.

"Jesus Aggie," Kirk says. "You okay?"

Patrick sits next to her on top of the table. He put his arm around her waist and she presses her face into his shoulder; this sound that she has never heard herself make escapes her mouth, and her shoulders sink. It's not a cry and it's not a laugh, not a sound she can quantify or even control, but a part of her that must have always been there. And she knows that that noise will still be inside of her, even when she doesn't remember how to make it, when she forgets that Patrick only smokes Lucky Strikes or can't even remember what Kirk sounds like when he calls her name from across the store.

Kirk makes a joke about Patrick's nicotine withdrawal already setting in, but none of them laugh.

"It's alright," Patrick says, resting his hand on the back of her head. Kirk sits on the other side of her, pulls a cigarette out for each of them, and squeezes her knee.

Kirk lights Patrick's cigarette, and they both suck sharply, a simultaneous inhale. Aggie thinks their breathing is a beautiful sound; she takes her hair down and removes the bandana, liking the way the air feels against her scalp.

Kirk hands her a cigarette. She presses it between her thumb and pointer finger, rolls it around there, and sucks too hard when Kirk lights it.

"Was that real?" she says.

"Yep," Patrick says. "And chaos killed the dinosaurs."

Kirk says, "I couldn't tell her I love her when I called to say we're alright."

Maybe there should be static electricity here, a hope that he has seen in her what he couldn't find before, but Agatha waits for it and feels none. She watches Kirk, pained as he hooks his toes under the bench of the table and stares at his feet.

"How does that happen?" Agatha asks. "I mean, you *did* love her."

"I did."

"So?"

Kirk just looks through her; because he can't explain it or because she wouldn't understand, she isn't sure.

"So," Patrick says, as if the word were somehow an explanation in itself. Agatha feels different from them but not alone.

"It's okay," she says; she watches the smoke, stagnant in the thick air. Maybe it's the buzz from the cigarette or the come down from the adrenaline, but suddenly, she feels more tired than she has ever been. She thinks about writing the truth in the bathroom, not in lipstick, or in ink, or in anything that could be erased, but really carving it in there with one of the pairing knives, pushing it until the drywall chips away: *Dear Howard, you can own almost nothing.* She puts out her cigarette and watches Patrick and Kirk do the same, thinking probably the idea will sound ridiculous tomorrow.

Mount Bonnell

My stepbrother, Will, is sitting in the chair that used to be my dad's favorite before he left, and he's smoking a joint and using a can of Diet Coke as an ashtray. He is talking about how the ego lives inside us all and creates pain, but nobody recognizes it because they are so possessed by it—or something like that. He keeps inhaling deeply and blowing all of the smoke out through his nose, and this is making me nervous because I know that my mom will flip out if she gets back from vacation and smells pot in the house.

Will's dad and my mom are on a kind of "second honeymoon." They've only been married for two years, but they are really into "celebrating their love" or whatever. They went to Hawaii, and Will and I are trapped in the suburbs of Austin for spring break, and I'm not old enough to drive, which means since Will is high, I am stuck here.

"I'm bored," I say, lying on the couch and pressing my face into a pillow to block out the smell of smoke.

"See Lex, that's exactly what I'm talking about. You're not bored, that's your ego talking. It's fueled by creating negative energy in your body. Here, smoke some of this," he says, leaning forward to offer me the joint. "Free yourself."

"I don't want to. It makes me feel sleepy. Besides, we shouldn't do it in the house."

"Don't be so constricted, Lex. You've only tried it twice."

"Isn't it restricted?" I say.

"Are you getting high or not?" he says.

I want to say not, but instead I say "fine" and let Will show me how to do it, even though I'm pretty sure that I have it down.

He puts his hand on my back, and I feel a jolt, like I'm falling fast but there is no ground to hit.

He moves closer to me, our bodies touching. "Just breathe and hold it in for a second and then exhale it," he says.

Will is a senior, and he and his friends smoke pot all the time, usually in the workshop in the garage that Will's dad never uses or sometimes at our high school, McCallum, in the "black hole," the lot that no one parks in because it's so far away.

Even though I'm a sophomore, smoking still kind of freaks me out. Once, at a party with Will, I smoked pot out of a pipe on someone's old trampoline, mostly just so I wouldn't look stupid, but it didn't make me laugh like everyone else. We were jumping, but I didn't feel exuberant like when I was a kid. I felt trapped, as if, no matter how bad I needed to, I'd never be able to come back down.

When my mom and I moved in with Will and his dad two years ago, I changed schools, and I haven't really made that many friends since. I'm kind of shy around people I don't know. At parties, I usually put on something short and try to blend in. Sometimes, I think I only really exist to Will.

"I don't want anymore," I say, after I've taken two hits.

Will puts a Radiohead CD in the stereo, and I pull my knees into my chest, press my head against them, and try to feel still.

Will sits beside me and covers me with one of the blankets from the couch. "Don't tense up like that," he says. "You okay?"

"Sleepy. I told you," I say, agitated. I stretch out on the couch. My eyes feel heavy, and my whole body feels light. I feel dizzy with anticipation, thinking about how it feels to fall.

"So sleep then," Will says.

"I don't want to."

"Call Kevin then."

"I told you, I don't like him," I say, for something like the fifth time that day.

"He wants to do it with you."

"Well I don't like him, and I wouldn't want him rolling around on top of me," I say, pulling the blanket over my head.

"That's the wrong way to describe it Lex," Will says. His laughing embarrasses me, but I start laughing too.

When the song changes, Will says, "Kevin's a jerk anyway. I never liked him."

Pot always makes him paranoid.

I fall asleep with Will's hand on my back. The smell of pot lingers in the air above us both, so thick I can taste it. The music from the stereo seems to fade away, and all I can hear is the sound of Will's breathing.

*

When we wake up, we are starving. Sonic is only right down the street, but we never go there because Will's mom used to take him there when he was a kid, and she died in a car-wreck on the way to work when

36

he was eight, and now, anything from Sonic makes him want to puke. That left ordering pizza or driving to Wendy's. We were too hungry to wait.

"Let's order pizza," Will says.

"Let's go to Wendy's," I say, not to disagree but because I love being in the car. I love rolling the windows down and pretending that I am actually headed somewhere.

"Okay fine, get some shoes on or something," he says.

In the car, Will always lets me pick the music, as long as it doesn't suck. He drives me to school every morning, which is much better than being driven by your parents.

At the stoplight on Anderson, Will doesn't look at Sonic. He never does. We talked about his mom and my dad once, and that was enough. My dad left when I was nine, and I've only seen him a couple of times since. He's remarried now to a woman named Julia who has two ugly Pomeranians.

When we get to Burnet, I say, "Let's keep driving."

The sun is right in our eyes, so Will wears his sunglasses. I like how disheveled he looks, with messy hair and the same white t-shirt from yesterday. In some ways, I want him to always stay the same.

"Where would we go?" he wants to know.

"Anywhere where nobody knows us."

"Yeah."

"Maybe somewhere with an ocean?"

Will reaches over and puts his hand on top of mine. "That's too far, Lex. We'd never make it back."

*

The first time Will and I did it, I was fourteen. It was last spring, and our parents were home, but their room is downstairs.

All through dinner that night, under the tablecloth, Will kept putting his foot on top of mine. It started out kind of like a joke, and then I took my foot and ran it down his leg and raised my eyebrows.

We had been flirting like that a lot lately. In the months before, we played this game where Will would pin me down and hold my arms above my head. We would wrestle or just stay like that, his weight pressing into me. It was just a game, but we never did it in front of our parents.

It was thundering outside that first night, and whenever that happened, I would go to Will's room, and we would usually just lie there and listen to it together. I wasn't as scared of it as Will thought I was, but I liked the way he would whisper *it's okay* when he thought I was afraid.

That night was different though because Will put his arm around me, and I turned around to face him, and he kissed me, and I kissed him back. We kissed hard and for a long time, the way I had wanted to for the whole year I had lived with him.

I had been reading my mother's *Cosmopolitans*, and I knew all about the things that guys could do to girls. Sometimes, lying on my stomach with my face hidden in my pillow, I would imagine Will doing those things to me, and I would shut my eyes and move my hand over my underwear until my heart sped up and I felt something contract inside of me and realized I had been holding my breath.

I kissed Will with my mouth open, the way you do when you've needed someone for a long time. We were touching each other, and I could feel his erection press against my stomach, solid and surprisingly warm. I was afraid to touch it, but I let him take off my underwear and put his fingers inside of me. It was so dark and every time it thundered, lightening filled the room. I pulled Will's bedspread over us and closed my eyes. I couldn't watch it.

Still, I took off my nightgown, and Will took off his boxers, and he kissed me all over. It tickled, but I didn't laugh. I kept forgetting to exhale, and over the thunder Will whispered, *Do you want to, Lex?*

I only got scared when I saw him putting on the condom because his thing looked bigger than I had realized and because the condom smelled strange. At first it really hurt and kind of stung, and I yelled *ouch* without even realizing it, and Will put his hand over my mouth so that we wouldn't wake up our parents.

Will kept telling me to relax, but I couldn't. I kept pulling away from him even though I didn't mean to, so he stopped. The condom had a little blood on it, which Will said he thought was normal. I still felt the stinging though, so I started crying a little. I didn't know it was going to hurt that bad, and Will kept asking me questions like what it felt like and how bad it hurt, but I didn't know how to explain it, which upset me more.

Will brought me my clothes and rubbed my back, and we stayed up until the thunder stopped, until we heard our parents' alarm.

At first I told myself that I would never do it again, but I kept being drawn to Will, like I couldn't find my balance and he was the one thing that could hold me up. We talked about stopping, but we never could.

Eventually it stopped hurting, and it even felt good. Then I couldn't stop thinking about it, and I would wait for thunderstorms.

Lately, we've stopped using storms as an excuse. We do it after-school before our parents get home or when they go out together for dinner. I still like it during thunderstorms though; my favorite way has always been in the dark.

*

After dinner, we swim in the pool and lay out in the sun. Under the water, everything feels weightless, and if I close my eyes, I can convince myself that I'm somewhere else. Sometimes, I come out here and swim at night. Floating on your back in the dark, you can almost forget everything about who you are.

"You should tan topless," Will says.

"No way, the neighbors might be home," I say, looking towards the fence covered in ivy that is twisting and tangling around itself.

"Your hair smells like apricots." He reaches over and draws imaginary pictures on my back with his finger. "You wanna do it?"

"Not right now," I say, turning over and shading my eyes from the sun.

I grab the copy of *Crime and Punishment* that I took from Will's backpack and suck in my stomach so that my chest rises. I undo my ponytail, letting my long dark hair fall over my shoulders.

"We can do it the way you like," Will says.

I know that he is thinking about me on top, know that he likes the way I look, but I just like it because I can bury my face in his shoulder.

He gets up and sticks his head into the water and then shakes his wet hair. The little drops fall on my stomach and arms and stay there, tiny little specks that sparkle in the sun.

"Hey, cut it out," I say, laughing. "Don't get this wet," I say, holding up his book. "I'm almost finished."

"Come on," he says, drying his wet hair with a towel. He has that look on his face that makes it impossible to ignore him.

"Fine," I say. "Then, will you take me somewhere?"

"Sure, anywhere you want."

*

Driving down 2222, Will says, "Are you sure this is where you wanna go?"

I love Mount Bonnell, but I think Will is secretly scared of heights. The peak is 780 feet high, but you can see the entire city from it.

Climbing the stone steps, Will says, "I should have asked you what you had in mind."

"Oh come on, it's not that bad; don't be so *constricted*," I say.

"Why are you so obsessed with this place anyway?" Will asks. He is already out of breath, but we have a long way to go before we make it to the top.

I like watching the sunset; it makes me feel something inside of myself that I am not afraid of.

I can't explain that though, so I just say, "I don't know" and tell him to hurry up or we'll miss it.

At the top of Mount Bonnell, I sit on the stone-wall that is meant to keep people from falling off the cliff.

"That makes me nervous," Will says. "Come here."

I won't move and Will knows this, so he puts his arms around me to keep me from falling.

"Want to hear a story?" I ask him.

The sun is about to start setting and then it will be dark. We are alone here, which is unusual because typically Mount Bonnell is busy at sunset.

Will doesn't answer.

"It's kind of a stupid story anyway," I say.

"That's okay," he says.

I can tell that he is in awe of this place. From so high up, you feel like you are in control. I tell him this place used to be called Antoinette's Leap.

"This girl, Antoinette, was engaged to a man she loved; I forget his name," I say. "But anyway, some Indians captured them, and he fought to the death to save her from them. Then, after the Indians killed him, she ran and made it all the way to the edge of this cliff. She heard the Indians catching up to her, so she took one look back at them and then jumped to her death."

"That's pretty crazy; who told you that?" Will asks, looking down at the cliffs below.

"My dad," I tell him. "People always say that she jumped to be with the guy though. That's why some people call this place lover's leap. Pretty dumb, right?" I say, even though I wish that Will would disagree.

Will nods, and we are quiet for a while.

"Why don't you stand behind the wall," he says. "You're kind of freaking me out."

"I'm not gonna fall," I say, turning over my shoulder to look at him. "I bet if I did, you wouldn't jump after me."

He smiles. "Not unless there were Indians chasing me."

At fifteen, I think that I am smart: that if I can expect less from people, then I can't be hurt by them. But standing there, I realize that I am always going to want more from Will. The sun sets in soft reds and yellows, oranges and pinks, and I lean against Will's chest and listen to him exhale and try not to think about what he said and what it meant.

"Don't you like it?" I ask.

Will has one arm around me and the other is shading his eyes from the sun. "Yeah."

"It makes me feel like we can't be wrong," I say, sitting and dangling my legs over the edge of the wall.

"We're not wrong," he says, squeezing my shoulders. "We just need to keep it a secret."

We watch the nighttime creep in over the sky, and I wish the lights of Austin would burn out so that, except for the stars, it would just be pitch black.

I want Will to hold me but not here. I want us to be somewhere else, anywhere where nobody knows us at all.

"What if—"

"They won't," Will cuts me off. "We're quiet."

He's right. We are always quiet. Even when we are alone.

"What do you think a black star looks like?"

"That's just a song, Lex. I don't even think there is such a thing."

"Maybe I mean a black hole then," I say.

"It looks like nothing. That's the point of them. They just suck in light and everything else. You wouldn't even know what hit you," he says. "Why do you wanna know about stuff like that?"

"Just want to."

"Get off the wall, would you?" he says irritably. "I should get you home. It's gonna rain."

"Let it rain. It's not gonna hurt us," I say, lying down on the wall, my hair falling over the edge.

"It's probably going to thunder," he tells me. Then, pulling at my arm he says, "You won't like that."

I take a breath and say, "Let's wait until it starts then."

We stay out there waiting for the rain, but it doesn't come. Instead there is just dark and stillness, the sound of cicadas in the distance, and wind that blows through our hair. I feel a lump rise in my throat, but I hold my breath because I don't trust myself to say the right thing.

I pick up a small rock that is next to me on the wall and throw it over the edge. We both watch it fall.

"Where's the storm?" I finally ask, sitting up. I am shivering, even though Will has his arms around me, and I can feel him pulling me tighter and tighter towards him, his legs on either side of me.

"Come on, it'll be okay," Will says.

"Why can't we stop?" I ask, but I let him put his hand on my thigh anyway, and I let him kiss me and lie on top of me on the wall, and when he does, I kiss him back hard, as if that alone can save us both.

"It's alright," Will says. I'm looking up at him, at the sky, dark behind him, and all I feel is really alone.

"Maybe," I say, even though I feel like everything might come undone.

"This is dangerous," Will says, surveying the cliffs below, as if he realizes for the first time that if either of us moves, we would both slip off the edge.

"I know," I say, and even though I am getting scared, I can hear myself whisper *Let's stay* because I know that I don't want to go home.

Acknowledgements

Thank you to the editors who previously published these stories: Roxane Gay, "Mount Bonnell," *[PANK]*; James McNulty, "You Could Stop It Here," *Driftwood Press*; and Gordon Krupsky, "The Last Dare," *The MacGuffin*. Tremendous gratitude to John Gosslee, Chris Campanioni, Ashley M. Jones, and Maya Marshall for all their time and energy invested in giving these words a home. Thanks also to Laura Metter for putting together the layout.

To good friends and readers: Corley Pillsbury, Cole Fowler, and Allie Mariano.

Thank you to McNeese State University for an invaluable three years and to my MFA family, especially Neil Connelly, Amy Fleury, Rita Costello, Emily Alford, Max Fisher-Cohen, Michael & Emily Shewmaker, Jonathan & Alison Pillow, Michael & Katie Rather, J & Sarie Fuller, Will & Missy Coppage, Janice Repka, Jason Reynolds, Jessica Hutchings, Becca & Dafydd Wood, Nancy Correro, Scott & Krista Thomason, and Erica McCreedy.

To my Midland College family for giving me both a teaching home and a writing life; thanks especially to Billy & Lori Feeler, Lynda Webb, Sara Peterson, and Pam Howell.

Thank you to Lindsay Hunter and Timothy Willis Sanders; I am grateful for your words of encouragement.

Sharon, Tim, Annie: love you always & forever.

Mom, Dad, Graham: it was a wild ride; your love and presence along the way meant, and still means, everything.

Brendan, I'm so happy and lucky to be living out the ellipsis with you. I love you.

The following stories have previously appeared in print:

"You Could Stop It Here"
appears in Volume 3, Issue 3 of *Driftwood Press.*
"The Last Dare"
appears in Volume 33, Issue 3 of *The MacGuffin.*
"Mount Bonnell"
appears in Volume 6, Issue 12 of *[PANK]*